K.S.L.

JUSTONENIGHT.COM BOOK 5

CHENCIA C. HIGGINS

TABLE OF CONTENTS

ALSO BY CHENCIA C. HIGGINS

<u>JustOneNight.com Novella Series:</u>

No Strings Allowed - Book 1

No Love Allowed - Book 2

The Week Before Forever – Book 2.5

No Games Allowed - Book 3

Holiday Honey – Book 4

K.S.L. – Book 5

<u>The Vow Series:</u>

To Buy a Vow – Book 1

To Build a Vow – Book 2

To Break a Vow – Book 3

Things Hoped For – Book 4

<u>Wolves of West Texas Series:</u>

Janine: His True Alpha – Book 1

Lenora: His Omega Mate – Book 2

Alicia: His Troublesome Fate – Book 3

<u>The Color Spectrum Duet:</u>

The Color Spectrum: Ebony

<u>Black Family Saga:</u>

Glasses

Fast Breaker

<u>The Luminous Cruse Chronicles:</u>

Love On The Luminous

<u>Boos & Booze</u>

Costume Cutty

<u>Standalones:</u>

Her & Them

Remember Our Love

Loud & Lew'd

Benefriends

An Illicit Seduction

Consolation Gifts

For the old dogs who thought it was too late to learn a new trick.

ONE

THE CATALYST

We were going to be late, but as much as I loved spending the holidays with my best friend and her husband, I was dreading the visit. An ill feeling settled in my stomach when I imagined having to hide the fact that I was no longer in love with my boyfriend of two years. My relationship with Blaine had run its course about six or twelve months ago, but being the stubborn Taurus that I was, I'd refused to admit defeat. I had no idea what Blaine's excuse was because he knew as well as I did that we were over.

Craning my neck, I glanced over my shoulder to peer at the analog clock mounted above the medicine cabinet. We should have been on the road to Quita and Simon's house over an hour ago. They only lived twenty minutes away from my apartment, but I'd been dragging from the moment my eyes popped open that morning. Still, I took my time rolling on my stockings, painstakingly dragging the material up my calves and over my knees. Somewhere in the back of my mind was the flawed logic that said, the longer I took to get there, the less time I'd have to be there. It was incredibly flawed because it completely ignored the very real possibility that Quita would insist that I stay after everyone was gone so that we could have more time together.

I sensed the moment that he appeared in the doorway of my bathroom and I tried not to cringe. The longer that I pretended that everything was fine with the two of us, the more I grew to resent him for doing the same. Aware of how my face was, without a doubt, broadcasting my wayward thoughts, I ignored Blaine's questioning gaze and stood, stretching the sheer fabric upward until it completely covered my hips and ass. After letting my skirt fall, I brushed my hands down my thighs, smoothing the wrinkles that only I could see, and turned to my boyfriend with a smile that likely looked as forced as it felt.

"Ready?" I asked brightly, feigning excitement.

It was a moot question since I already knew the answer. Blaine still hadn't said a word, but I could feel the tension in the room as if it were a third person.

Holding my gaze, Blaine licked his lips, and I sucked in a breath. *Was this it? Was this the moment?* Suddenly, I was hit by a wave of nerves, and the last thing I wanted to do was have this conversation. *Who knew I was such a coward?*

"I—" he began, but quickly broke off with a shake of his head as I walked past him to enter the bedroom.

Interrupting him while he did what I'd been too stubborn to do was rude, but I had to get out of the tiny confines of my bathroom. I needed room to breathe if we were going to have that conversation. Leaving his post in the doorway, Blaine crossed the bedroom and stood in front of me. As I stared up at him, my heart thudded in my chest, and when he reached for both of my hands, the blood began roaring in my ears. He peered down at me, his pale brown eyes full of apprehension as they searched mine.

"Malina, I'm sorry, baby, but I can't do this anymore. I don't want to hurt you, but this just isn't working. I can't go to this Friendsgiving and pretend that everything is fine with us. I'm *so* sorry, baby." He squeezed my hands in his as he waited for me to respond, the apprehension he'd been wearing now replaced with hope.

A sensation similar to a balloon popping happened in my chest, and I released a heavy breath. The relief I felt was almost overwhelming.

Smiling softly, I offered a cautious nod. "No, you're right. Something has been off for a while. I'm glad it's not just me."

His brows shot up, and for a moment he appeared startled, but then he shook it off and returned my smile. "Oh, okay. So..." he trailed off, and it seemed like he was once again waiting on me.

"So?" I prompted, nodding slowly, unsure of what he was trying to say.

"Yeah. So."

I lifted an eyebrow. "So...we're breaking up, right? That's where you were going with this?"

"Only if that's what you want."

Frowning, I shook my head. "You just said you 'couldn't do this anymore', so regardless of whether or not I felt the same, this would end. I'm not trying to hold on to someone who feels like they have to pretend to still be in love with me."

Now he was the one frowning. He dropped my hands and took a step back.

"I never said I wasn't in love with you anymore."

Propping my hands on my hips, I tilted my head

to the side and pinned him with a knowing look. "Well, are you?"

We stared at each other in silence for a few minutes before he threw his hands up in the air and turned to go back into the ensuite bathroom.

"That's not the point, Malina!" He yelled over his shoulder. It wasn't lost on me how he'd avoided giving me a straight answer.

Instead of yelling at his back, I sat on the uphol- stered bench at the foot of my bed and crossed my legs while I waited. When he reappeared in the door- way, he held the body wash he'd used the night before, a toothbrush, and the small bottle of cologne that I'd bought for his birthday three months earlier. He stopped in front of me before sighing loudly and shaking his head. Then he continued into the living room without saying a word. My jaw dropped open, and I hopped up out of my seat and rushed after him. He was in the living room, standing over the couch as he placed the items he'd taken out of my bathroom inside of a box.

"What is this?" I asked him incredulously, gesturing at the cardboard that was no larger than two shoe boxes stacked on top of one another.

"These are my things."

Moving to stand at his elbow, I peered down into the box and saw that it was, indeed, filled with his things. There were a couple of undershirts, some boxers, and a few grooming products. And in the corner of the medium box was an industrial-sized bottle of cocoa butter. The sight of it all rendered me speechless, and for a moment, I just stared at it.

"Wow," I uttered when I could finally find the words to speak. "You weren't kidding around."

He shifted his weight from one foot to the other and shoved his hands in his pockets. "Well...no, but neither were you."

Snapping my gaze to his face, I gave him a disbelieving look. "Except I haven't already gone to your apartment and packed up all of my things without even speaking to you!"

Seemingly exasperated, Blaine tossed his hands up in the air, and I took a reflexive step back from him, putting a few feet of space in between us.

"You don't have any things at my place to begin with! You never even go to my place. We're always here in *your* apartment."

"Why are you saying it as some sort of accusation?" I questioned incredulously. "Did we not agree to spend most of our time over here?"

It was something we'd just sort of fell into at the beginning of our relationship, right around the time we regularly began having sex. I lived closer to our friends, and it just made more sense to be at my place. Besides, I hated Blaine's apartment. He had the barest of minimums when it came to furniture, and he never had a decent amount of food in his refrigerator or cupboards. He had the odds and ends of snacks and various take-out containers, but what was there was never enough to create an appetizing meal. After my second sleepover at his house, I'd decided that I was already tired of having to order in every single time, and I didn't like having to bring a blanket and pillow with me. Even Blaine had mentioned the difference when he spent the night over at my place for the first time.

"You have so many pillows!" he exclaimed, his voice full of admiration. "And they're so soft and they smell good." Then, he swept all of those pillows onto the floor, and we made love on top of the freshly-laundered duvet that covered my queen bed.

But now, I stared up at him, wondering if maybe he had only pretended that it wasn't a big deal for us to primarily spend our time at my apartment because he could tell how much I didn't want to go to his. The fact that it was a possibility made me want to cut the argument short. Immediately, I shook my head and grabbed one of his hands in mine.

"You know what? It doesn't matter. None of that matters anymore. What matters now is that we're cordial with one another so that we can maintain our friendship."

And I meant that. Blaine and I had been friends for more than a year before our relationship changed from platonic to romantic. We would meet up with or without our friend group to catch a movie or have lunch. I knew that with the end of our romantic relationship, things wouldn't immediately go back to that, but I hoped that we could get there eventually.

Without hesitation, Blaine nodded and pulled me into a hug, wrapping his arms around my waist, and resting his forehead on top of my head. The hug was comfortable, like second nature for us, and the familiarity of it made me smile.

"You're right," he agreed, "we were friends before this, and we'll be friends afterward."

I nodded as he stepped away from me.

"So, this is it? We're officially over?"

Skepticism coated every word as they dripped out of his mouth. When I dipped my chin in confirmation, he blew another breath out of his mouth.

"*Wow.* Well, we had a good run."

"We did," I agreed with a shrug, "and things were really great there for a while but…"

"…now they aren't," he finished. Tilting my head back, I stared at him, chewing on my bottom lip. "Walk me out?" he requested.

"Of course."

Nibbling on my lower lip, I watched as Blaine lifted the box into his hands, then we both headed to the front door, where I stepped into a pair of ballet flats before walking him out into the parking lot. He placed the box on the floor between the backseat and the passenger seat, shut the door, and turned to face me. I didn't know what to say, so we just stood there looking at each other as awkwardness swirled around us.

After a moment of silence that stretched longer than it should, Blaine sighed and dropped his eyes to the ground before raising them to meet my gaze.

"I'm probably not going to make it to the Friendsgiving."

Surprised, my brows immediately shot up. That was unexpected. "*Oh*. Okay. Well, happy Thanksgiving. Um…" I fiddled with the hem of my blouse. "I guess…this is good-bye?"

Frowning, Blaine shook his head. "What? No. This isn't goodbye. This is 'see you later'. Okay?"

I heard what he was saying, but it didn't *feel* like that was the truth. There was a crackle in the air filled with underlying discontent but I didn't know how to eradicate it, so I stood there and chewed on the corner of my bottom lip, ruining the lipstick that I had applied only thirty minutes earlier.

"Okay. Well, see you later."

"Right." He replied slowly, clearly feeling the same unpleasantness as me. "Just…not later today."

Pressing my lips together, I fought not to roll my eyes. *Was it even necessary to add that last part?*

"Okay, Blaine. Drive safe." I started to step away from him so that he could cross over to the driver's side and climb in his car, but he grabbed my wrist, effectively holding me in place. Trailing my eyes up from his hand, I found that the awkwardness on his face was gone.

"What's up?"

He leaned toward me, his eyes narrowed and brows lowered, contorting his face into the picture of a concerned friend. "Hey, I debated whether or not to say something, but because we're friends, I couldn't not."

A sudden rush of anxiety hit me in the chest. "What?" I whispered beseechingly. "What is it?"

"Well," he began in a lowered tone, as if he were sharing top secret information with me, "you're kind of…terrible…at sucking dick, and you should probably think about that before you jump into your next relationship."

When he finished speaking, he released another breath—this one full of relief, as if he'd been holding onto that little tidbit for far too long and was grateful to *finally* have the weight of that secret lifted off his chest—and then straightened and offered me a friendly smile. From the easy curve of his lips, you'd think he just told me that blizzards were two-for-one at Dairy Queen. You wouldn't believe that he'd just dropped a steaming bag of dog shit on my feet. Dumbfounded, I gaped at him, but either he couldn't read my expression, or—more likely—he just didn't give a fuck, because he leaned forward and pressed a platonic kiss on my forehead. Releasing me from his grasp, he didn't say another word as he crossed to the other side of his vehicle and climbed behind the steering wheel.

I stood there, shocked into silence, while he stuck his left arm out of the window and tossed me a friendly wave before pulling out of the parking lot and exiting my apartment complex.

TWO

ENROLLMENT

"He. Said. What?!"

Stabbing my fork into the thick slice of sweet potato pie on the plate in front of me, I shoved it in my mouth before nodding morosely.

"Yep," I grumbled around the dessert.

"What does that even *mean*?" Quita murmured, her eyes on the wall in front of us.

We were sitting at the rectangular table in her dining room. I'd waited until dinner was over and everyone had headed into the den to watch the parade, before pulling Quita aside and telling her the news. She hadn't been surprised to hear that Blaine and I had split, but when I mentioned his parting words, she exploded.

Assuming that her question was rhetorical, I

shrugged and stuffed another forkful of pie into my mouth.

"I mean," Quita continued, "if that was even really true, why would he wait until right then to tell you? Why not say something early on in your relationship, when you have an opportunity to do something about it?" Suddenly, she gasped and turned to me, gripping my forearm tightly.

"Oh my gosh!" she exclaimed. "Is that why he broke up with you? Because you're terrible at head? What a piece of shit!"

Quita ranted on, calling Blaine every name in the book. It didn't seem like she was looking for a response, so I didn't even bother trying to get a word in edgewise, instead, nodding my agreement as I drained my third glass of wine and focused on devouring my second slice of pie. Quita's husband, Simon, did all of the baking for the Friendsgiving that they hosted, and I looked forward to his pies all year. In fact, when Blaine informed me that he wouldn't be coming to the event Quita and Simon had held for the past four years, I felt a small measure of gratitude that I wouldn't miss out on the pie. Distantly, I understood that being worried about dessert while ending a relationship was a red flag but, at this point, it didn't really matter.

This group of friends was actually how Blaine

and I had met. Quita and I had been ace boons since middle school, long before she met the man who would eventually become her husband. A year after they married, they ditched the tradition of bouncing from home to home during the holidays and started their own tradition, inviting their close friends into their home to break bread with. On Simon's shortlist of friends was Blaine, who he'd first met in under-grad and reconnected with when they both ended up working at Franklin University. Simon was a department dean, and Blaine was an account representative in administration. Of course, I was at the top of Quita's list.

From the moment that Blaine and I met, we'd hit it off. Things between us had been effortless from the beginning. We liked most of the same things, and truly enjoyed each other's company. I couldn't even pinpoint when things changed because, in truth, *nothing* had changed. He was still the same guy that he'd been when I met him four years ago and, as far as I knew, I was still the same woman.

Maybe that was it. Perhaps we were stagnant. Although things were good, there was no growth, and since there was no growth, the love had nowhere to go, so it died. The end of the relationship didn't have to be a bad thing. We hadn't even had sex in over a month. I didn't feel any animosity about it and from the way he hadn't brought it up, I could only assume he was fine with the drought as well. As they said—whoever *they* were—all good things must come to an end, and as Blaine had said—we'd had a good run.

Except for the minor fact that I apparently gave trash head.

Groaning, I reached across the table to grab the pitcher of spiked sweet tea that had been left behind after the table was cleared when everyone finished dinner. Topping off my wine glass with the dark brown beverage, I sat back in my chair and sipped on the tea, deep in thought. The worst part about all of this was that Blaine was right. I *was* terrible at sucking dick. I just...wasn't good at it, and Blaine hadn't been interested in me wasting my time with my head in his lap. It seemed like it was more of a waste of *his* time, and I'll never forget the way I felt when he'd pushed my head away and told me not to worry about it.

He hadn't been rude—he didn't mush me and tell me to get the fuck away from him—but the tone of his voice had haunted me for a while after that. He just sounded so...disgusted, and that hurt my feelings for weeks. But then I saw the silver lining in the situation and realized that I was, in truth, getting the long end of the stick. If Blaine didn't want me to suck his dick then I never had to come up with an excuse not to do it. I was hashtag winning.

For the two years that Blaine and I were together, I'd only had to suffer through three attempts to suck his dick before he put a stop to it. After I realized the blessing I'd been dealt, I never thought of it again. Now, thanks to his parting last words, it was weighing heavily on my mind. I couldn't stop thinking about it, and I was more upset about the fact that he'd thrown that in my face than I was by the fact that we'd broken up.

Sliding my eyes over to my friend, who was still fussing and cussing, it occurred to me that maybe Blaine had anticipated Quita's reaction to the news of our splitting up. It would explain why he had chosen to go to his family's house instead of coming to the Friendsgiving first and then going over there as we'd done for the past two years.

"Why the hell would he tell you to 'think about that' before getting into your next relationship?!" Quita snapped. "As if every man cares about that kind of thing? *He* didn't care about it, so why would he do that to you?"

"Apparently, he did care about it," I mumbled over the rim of my glass. *Why else would he say it if he didn't?*

"If he *truly* cared about it," she fumed, dark eyes blazing with rage, "he should have helped you improve. *Not* stay silent on it for two years, and then tell you when he's breaking up with you. Because what are you supposed to do with that information now? It's not like there are any schools out there for dick sucking. There's not any website where you can log on to take a master class from Superhead, where sis can tell you exactly what you're supposed to do. Is World Star even still around for you to find that infamous video with the woman that sounds like Daffy Duck?"

Thinking of the video in question, I busted out laughing, my shoulders shaking and cheeks hurting from how hard I was laughing. I definitely could've benefited from either of those right then.

"There's a reason that stuff isn't a thing!" continued Quita. "Giving head isn't something you can learn how to do by watching a video. And you can't use props either, because a rubber banana ain't gon' tell you if you're using too much teeth! You need the real thing, beloved."

The moment that she said that, a lightbulb clicked on in my head, and I instantly knew what I needed to do. I snapped my fingers and placed my glass back on the table.

"That's it! That's what I have to do!"

Quita gave me a weird look. "What are you talking about, girl?"

"I gotta get the real thing!" I nodded eagerly, a plan already forming in my mind.

She just stared at me.

Ignoring her, I sat up straight, my leg bouncing from my excitement. "I'm going to use the same website that you used to get your husband, and I'm gonna find me a man that I can practice sucking dick on."

Still silent, Quita began blinking rapidly.

"Well?" I prompted, wondering if I'd broken her. "Say something."

She cleared her throat. "Um…you know that me and Simon were a fluke right? JustOneNight.com isn't a website you use to find a husband. It's explicitly for fucking."

Pursing my lips, I gave her a flat look. "Duh! I know that, girl. I'm not looking for a husband. Hell, I'm not even looking for a damn boyfriend. I just got rid of mine, remember?" Shrugging, I added, "I'm trying to fuck a man with my mouth."

Gasping, her eyes widened, making me laugh. "Don't look all scandalized, Quita. You just said so yourself that you met your husband on a fucksite, so don't judge me for wanting to use the site for its intended purpose."

Shaking her head, she lifted a hand. "I'm not judging you, heifer. I'm just…concerned."

I frowned. "What are you concerned about?"

Instead of answering me, Quita grabbed the nearly empty pitcher of spiked tea and moved it out of my reach, then she turned to me.

"I'm concerned that you're drunk and saying things out of hurt. You just broke up with your boyfriend, whom you loved, and now you're trying to figure out what to do with those emotions. I just don't want you to make a rash decision based on how you feel right now."

Blowing a breath out through my nose, I rolled my eyes. Quita meant well, but she was way off base. "I'm not hurt because Blaine and I split up, Quita. I'm hurt that Blaine let me walk around for two years, *knowing* that my mouth game was Playskool level and never told me."

"Okay…" Quita began slowly, pinning me with a shrewd look, "was it a complete shock when he said that to you? Did you honestly have absolutely no idea that your head was trash?"

Face scrunched, I stared at the woman who I thought was my best friend, but was apparently a damn traitor. "Wow, Quita! Really?!"

Her lips twitched, and I could tell that she was trying to hold back a laugh. "I'm serious," she insisted. "I'm genuinely asking if you had no idea. I'm not trying to imply anything." Leaning toward me, she propped her chin on my shoulder. "I promise."

Huffing, I sat back and folded my arms across my chest, but didn't shake her off of me.

"No, it wasn't a surprise when he said that to me. I knew."

Likely expecting that answer, Quita nodded, the sharp point of her bony chin digging into the meat of my shoulder. "Right, so if you already knew, why are you so hurt?"

Twisting my lips to the side, I stared at the wall across the room and admitted to myself that it was a good question. One I needed to reflect on, instead of immediately trying to deflect by defending my feelings. I sat in those feelings for a few minutes and tried to figure out how I wanted to answer her. Thankfully, Quita gave me the space to do that, waiting quietly for me to speak. Finally, I shifted in the chair and cleared my throat.

"Maybe...hurt was the wrong word to use, even though you used it first." I glanced at her from the corner of my eye to see her eyes roll as she pursed her lips. "I guess I'm more...embarrassed."

"And angry?" she suggested gently.

Instantly, I nodded, glad that she got it. "Definitely angry. I'm angry about the way he threw that in my face when we were parting, as if it was the last jab for the technical win in a boxing match. I mean, he'd played it off for *two years*, convincing me that it was no big deal, but the way he said it proved that it was obviously an issue for him." My anger flared and I clenched my hands into fists, my short nails digging into my palms.

"That he didn't say anything until we were already over—had literally *just* decided to call it quits—let me know that he didn't want me to be better at it because he didn't want to be with me." I glanced at Quita to see her face scrunched in consternation. "What I'm saying is, he knew within the first few months of us being together that giving head wasn't my strong suit. I could ride dick like it was a mechanical bull, but when it came to using my mouth, the skills just weren't there. If he'd planned for us to be together long term—I mean beyond two years—then I would think he'd have invested the time into making sure that was something I could do right, or at least done in a way that it pleased him. He would make sure that every part of our lovemaking was enjoyable for him. Right?"

I turned to her for confirmation. "Wouldn't that make sense?" She nodded, but her face held mild skepticism. I shook my head. "But he didn't. He held his tongue until right before the bell rang, and *that* let me know that he had no intentions of us being together for long."

"Damn," Quita murmured, "that's fucked up."

And yeah, she was right about that, but also, "Eh. I knew that we didn't need to be together as long as we were and yet I held my tongue as well." I couldn't put all the blame on him. There was also some culpability lying at my feet.

Quita sat up, pinning me with a hard look. "*You* were silent when you should have been calling for an end to your relationship. I could tell you weren't in it for the long haul, but I wasn't going to be the one to piss on your parade. However, I know damn well that you would *not* have held your tongue if he couldn't eat the box like he was the motherfucking Glizzy Gladiator!"

Bobbing my head, I immediately agreed. "Now that's a damn fact! That's something that would have been rectified immediately, or we wouldn't have made it to two years, because that's not going to work for your girl." I sighed, deflating a little. "Obviously, Blaine doesn't think the same way."

Quita waved her hand. "Man, fuck Blaine."

Grinning, I nodded again because Quita was my girl. Blaine was one of her husband's good friends, and yet she still had solidarity with me and I loved her for that.

"Been there, done that. Now, it's on to the next."

The scowl on her face melted away, and that concern reappeared in her eyes.

"Okay, I hear you, but the next doesn't have to happen *right now*. Honestly, it probably shouldn't happen for a while."

"What the hell do you mean *a while*?" I demanded, sharply, jerking my neck to the side to give her a crazy look. "Am I supposed to sit here and be single for the next two years just to make up for our failed relationship?"

"What? No! That's not what I'm saying at all. What *I'm* saying is that you should probably take a break. I know that you'd checked out on Blaine a long ass time ago, but that doesn't mean you don't need to grieve the loss of your relationship. Give it a little time before you jump on that next baloney pony."

I tilted my head from side to side as if I was weighing her words in my mind. "Well, you'll be happy to know that I'm not looking to jump on any ponies anytime soon. I *am* trying to work on my mouth though."

"Malina," Quita began, chastisement weighing down her tone, but I interrupted her.

"No, girl. Let's go to your office so I can set me up an account and find me someone who's going to help me ensure that the next man I call mine won't be able to say that shit to me—or anybody else—if we break up."

I fixed my gaze on her, waiting to see what she was going to do. She didn't say anything for a minute, staring back at me as if she expected me to change my mind. I raised my eyebrows and she finally heaved a resigned sigh, pushing back from the table.

"Okay, come on."

Pleased, I clapped my hands excitedly and stood to follow her through the house. Once we stepped into her office, she closed the door and directed me to sit in the chair at her desk. The signup process didn't take long at all, maybe about twenty minutes total, with the bulk of that time spent waiting for the background check to come back. Quita didn't say much while I was setting up my profile, outside of offering suggestions here and there, but she became incredibly vocal when she saw what I put in the box labeled "about me".

"Hell no!" she screeched, standing over my shoulder with her eyes on the screen.

Ignoring her, I moved on to my likes and dislikes.

Reaching over me, she grabbed my hand, stilling the mouse.

"Are you insane?"

I looked back at her, my brows furrowed. "Why I gotta be all that, Quita?"

Narrowing her eyes, she glared at me before turning back to the screen and reading what I'd written aloud.

"*All you need to know is that I'm here to suck some dick. No penetration needed except for your penis in my mouth.*"

She finished and stared at me, but I just shrugged.

"What? It's straight to the point."

Quita groaned. "You might as well type 'harass me' in all caps if you're just going to put something like that up there."

"I thought you said there was little to no harassment on this website." I reminded her. "You said that the amount of creeps on this website was fantastically low because JustOneNight does extensive background checks on every user." I narrowed my eyes at her. "Were you just lying to me when you said that? Or…" I trailed off, waiting for her to confirm or deny.

Annoyed, she huffed, "No, heifer, I wasn't lying when I said that. This is basic dating app etiquette. It's for the creeps who'll see your picture and immediately slide into your messages talking about," she dropped her voice to imitate a man's register, "them lips look like they'd be right at home around my dick." She gave me a pointed look, but I still didn't see the problem.

"Quita," I said slowly, hoping that she would understand, "that type of nigga sounds like the exact person I'm looking for. I *want* to wrap my lips around somebody's dick." Tapping my temple, I asked, "What's not clicking?"

"Oh my God," she muttered to herself before releasing my hand and backing away from the desk slowly. She raised her hands into the air as a sign of surrender and shook her head.

"You got it, man. I don't know where to go from here, so I'mma just let you do your thing. When you're done, let me know."

"I'm done," I assured her. "They don't need to know much more than what I already added. All I have left to do now is upload a picture, which you said I can do through the app."

I pulled my phone out of my pocket and navigated to the app marketplace. Quita walked me through downloading the JustOneNight app on my phone so that I could keep up with messages while we went back into the rest of the house. I snapped a selfie, did a quick edit on the picture, and uploaded it onto my profile.

"Seriously, Malina?" Quita fussed, sounding particularly exasperated when she saw the image. It was a close-up of my mouth. My lips, which were painted a deep, cherry-red, were just barely pursed and the focal point of the image.

"Yeah, girl," I responded, lifting one shoulder nonchalantly. "They don't need to see my body. Hell, they don't even need to see my whole face. All they need is this six inches of space between my nose and my neck."

"I cannot *wait* to see this," she murmured as we left her office.

We'd just made it back to the kitchen so that I could grab another slice of pie when my phone chimed. Quita rushed to my side while I pulled out the device to see that I already had a notification from the JustOneNight app.

"You have a message already!" Quita exclaimed, her voice now full of excitement.

I couldn't lie; I was feeling it a little too. Pressing the notification, I bit my lip as I waited for the message to pop up, only for my face to fall when it did.

"*What the hell*," Quita muttered as I stared at the message for a moment before I busted out laughing.

It consisted of two words and a picture. "Eat me," and a dick pic.

"See!" Quita squealed, slapping my bicep. "I told you!"

Unperturbed, I shrugged. That wasn't too bad. It was a surprisingly decent-looking dick; at least six inches, if but a tad ashy. I received two more pictures before someone named Rhone broke up the chain. His message was one question.

Rhone: Is this a prank?

Snickering, I immediately typed out a reply.

Me: Why would I pay a steep membership fee just to pull a prank?

Rhone: I've seen some wild stuff on social media. It's not too far-fetched.

I laughed. He had a point.

Me: That's not what I'm on. This is legit.

Rhone: That's what's up. So, what're your criteria? How are you deciding who to go with?

Me: How big is your dick?

Quita slapped my arm again. "Now you're *soliciting* dick pics?! Have you no shame?"

The look I gave her called her an ignorant hood-possum, since she was over thirty and had passed the qualifying age for being a hood rat.

"I told however many thousand people on this website that I'm tryna give a random man a mouth hug. What is shame, beloved? I don't know her."

Smirking, she rolled her eyes. "I guess you're right."

Before I could respond, my phone chimed again. We both peered down at the screen to see that Rhone had replied to my query. Instead of words, he'd responded with a picture of his left hand making the OK sign. It wasn't a complete circle since his thumb and index finger were about half an inch apart, but a grin burst onto my face. I didn't really have a sense of what I was looking for when I came up with this idea, but I knew that the men who had contacted me before Rhone weren't it. I liked the fact that he hadn't sent me his dick, even though I'd basically asked for it. More than that, when I zoomed in on the picture, I could see that his nails were clean and smooth, and his cuticles looked healthy. That stood out to me, telling me more about him than a dick pick could have.

Rhone was the one.

"Damn," Quita murmured, sounding slightly disappointed, "I thought for sure he was about to slide another ashy selfie into your inbox."

I chuckled as I responded to Rhone's message.

Me: Interesting.

Rhone: I can't be giving you all the goods upfront. A man has to leave something to the imagination.

Biting my lip, I tried to keep from laughing but it didn't work.

Me: You're funny.

Rhone: You didn't say funny was a requirement, so I can't tell if that's a good thing or not.

Me: I haven't decided.

Rhone: Alright. Let me know when you find out.

Nibbling on the corner of my lips, I thought about what I wanted then I typed out a reply.

Me: You busy tomorrow night?

THREE

ORIENTATION

The following night, I found myself standing outside a red-painted door inside of a boutique hotel that was located in Third Ward. Although this whole arrangement had been my idea, my stomach roiled, and my mouth was dry. I was nervous as hell and had been questioning myself all day. Drunk me had seen the logic in this, but sober me wondered why it even mattered.

You're kind of…terrible…at sucking dick.

Blaine's words echoed in my brain, giving me the push I needed. Although he'd never been cruel while we were together, Blaine had undoubtedly said it to hurt me, and the bullet had met its target. The intimacy between us had been an important part of our union. We'd waited a few months before going all-in because, even though our relationship was built on our friendship, we wanted to be sure that the sex wasn't a driving factor. For me, it hadn't been. I'd genuinely enjoyed being with Blaine...until I didn't. When I took his parting words into account, it became apparent that avoiding the inevitable was just another thing we'd had in common. But that was over now.

Straightening my back, I shored up my resolve and pressed the tiny, round button beneath the number plate mounted in the center of the door. The sharp buzz it elicited caused me to jump, even as I was the one who set the sound in motion. Within seconds, the door opened, as if the person on the other side had been standing there, waiting for me to announce my arrival. The man I presumed to be Rhone stood in front of me, a warm smile on his handsome face.

"You must be Malina," he stated in a smooth voice that caused a ripple of tingles to run across my shoulders.

Smiling, I offered a quick nod of acknowledgment. "Yes. Good evening, Rhone."

"Please, come in." He stepped back and to the side, widening the door to allow me entrance into the room. "You're beautiful," he said matter-of-factly, peering at me from behind rectangular frames that gave him a studious air as I walked past him and made my way over to the seating area near the window.

The compliment—and the surety in his voice as he issued it—made me smile. It was unexpected, considering what we were about to do, but it was nice to hear all the same. I had taken the time to make sure I looked good for the night; even though in the back of my mind I knew it really didn't matter. I'd styled my long locs in Bantu knots the night before so that when I unraveled them, they hung around my face in deep waves. I wore a calf-length pencil skirt which, when paired with the four-inch heels I'd chosen, put me right at five-nine and made my ass look fantastic, and a long-sleeved, silk blouse that tied at my neck in an elaborate bow. My lips were painted a deep red, and my eyelashes were separated and curled after a couple of swipes of mascara. I topped it all off with a few dabs of my favorite essential oil on my wrists and behind my ears.

"Thank you," I responded as I ran my eyes over his frame.

Unlike me, Rhone had a couple of full-body photos on his profile. Quita and I had studied those pictures endlessly, so I already knew what he looked like, but seeing him in person was another thing entirely. He was a few inches taller than me in my heels, with a heft in his long arms, thick legs, and belly that assured me he wasn't a lightweight. Both his warm brown skin and the thick beard that covered the bottom half of his face looked sufficiently moisturized, and his hair was brushed into low waves. A sliver of my nerves was eased when I noted that he had also chosen to dress nicely. He wasn't wearing standard booty-call attire, and that validated my chosen outfit. His stout frame was attractively wrapped in gray slacks and a black button-down, which was tucked into his pants and secured by a black, leather belt. He watched me with intelligent, dark brown eyes which seemed amplified by those wide, black frames.

"You can have a seat," he offered, gesturing at the wingback chair behind me.

He waited until I sat down before sitting in the center of the small couch opposite the chair. A low table separated us, but it didn't seem like enough, and once we were both seated, my heart began to pound with the nerves I thought I'd left at the door.

I'd brought my behind all the way here to put a stranger's dick in my mouth. My mama would've been scandalized if she knew. Perched on the edge of the chair, I linked my hands over my knees which were pressed together tightly to keep them from knocking.

Neither of us said a word; we just stared at each other. He had such nice lips; thick, brown, and moisturized like the rest of him. *Hopefully,* that extended to the part of him that I came to see. I'd find out as soon as I figured out a tactful way to tell him to pull his dick out. Quita hadn't given me any tips on how these types of hookups were supposed to go—mostly because she felt a way about me doing this so soon after Blaine.

While I was in my head and observing Rhone, his brows rose over the rim of his glasses, but he still didn't say anything, simply giving me a curious look that I couldn't decipher. After a couple of minutes went by, he shook his head and held up his hands.

"Hey. I know we agreed to do this, but it's okay if you've changed your mind since last night. I won't be upset."

Twisting my lips to the side, I peered at him in confusion. "You…don't want me to suck your dick?" With my hands in my lap, I tugged on my fingers to keep from covering my face. I couldn't believe I'd said something so wild to man I didn't know.

Chuckling, Rhone shook his head again. "I'd love to have you suck my dick, however, the vibes I'm feeling from you say that you're uncomfortable, which is making me uncomfortable in turn. You seem nervous as if you don't want to be here, and I'm starting to feel like Chris Hansen is going to pop out with a microphone and ask me if I knew you were thirteen-years-old when we set this up. So, we can just part ways. It's okay. I promise."

The sincerity in his eyes made me release the breath that I'd been holding. It was time to lay all of the cards on the table, which was another thing that Quita had insisted I do from the beginning. She wasn't trying to hear me explain that no man was going to hook up with a woman to get a subpar blow job on purpose. She'd told me to have a little faith in men, and I'd told her that she was biased because Simon was a great guy. Quita was five years removed from the struggle of navigating men while single; her opinion was invalid.

"Okay, let me be straight with you," I began, my eyes fixed on Rhone's deep brown gaze. "The complete reason that I'm here is that I broke up with my boyfriend yesterday, and right before he left, he told me that my head was trash. Everything before that was cordial and kind but that was not and I can't just let it go. So, I'm here because I want to learn how to not have trash head, so that the next man I'm with can say that he has no idea what my ex was talking about."

Rhone stared at me unblinkingly, and I covered my face in embarrassment. He'd probably never had such an egotistical proposition before and was likely trying to decide the nicest way to make his exit. Since this was my grand idea, I offered to make things easy for him.

"I'm sorry for not telling you the truth upfront," I mumbled into my hands before blowing out another resigned breath and meeting Rhone's eyes. "If you want to leave, I'll completely understand." I'd turned his words on him, but they carried a different weight with the full story hanging between us.

His eyebrows knitted and he shook his head. "Nah. You wanted me here, so I'm here. Besides, just because your ex said your head game is trash doesn't make it true."

Snorting, I crossed my ankles and leaned my legs to one side, propping my head on my fist as I balanced an elbow on the arm of the chair. "As much as I hate to admit it, he was telling the truth." I'd never had a problem giving Blaine his props, but this was one bitter pill to swallow.

Rhone made a non-committal sound, as if he didn't quite believe me, and shrugged. "Show me."

Straightening, I dropped my hands to my lap and stared at him. A smile slowly bloomed on my face as hope did the same in my chest. "Seriously?"

He dipped his chin once and then tilted his head

to the side, beckoning me to him. "Yeah. Come over here and show me what you're working with."

I didn't hesitate. Reaching into my small clutch, I grabbed one of the condoms I'd brought with me and walked around the table to stand in front of him. Using his foot, Rhone pushed the low table away from the sofa and closer to the chair, giving me plenty of room to sink to my knees in front of him. He spread his legs and I inched closer, gripping his knees, my eyes on the bulge below his belt. When he didn't move, I lifted my gaze to his face. His bottom lip was clenched between his teeth and his eyes were on me. He was giving me that curious look again and my belly fluttered with nerves.

"Are you gonna pull it out?"

One of his eyebrows rose. "Is that what you want me to do?"

"Uh, how else am I gonna suck it?"

"Why don't you just do what you would normally do?"

Huffing out a breath, I rolled my eyes. "I don't normally do anything. That's why I'm here!"

Rhone shook his head, his brown eyes trained on me. "No. You're here because your ex told you that you were bad at something, and now you want to prove him wrong."

I shrugged. "That sounds like the same thing to me."

"I beg to differ."

Annoyed, I glared at him. This was a whole lot of back and forth for what should have been cut and dry.

"It seems like you're being difficult on purpose. Do you want this or not? Because there were at least four other men in my messages that I can reach out to."

"I apologize if it seems like I'm being difficult. You said you wanted help so that's what I'm trying to provide. Unless you show me your technique, I don't know how to guide you. Imagine this was a math problem on a test and you were marked wrong. I would need you to demonstrate the steps you took to get your answer so that I can see where you went wrong and correct your process."

Ah. His analogy made perfect sense and I felt my irritation melt away. Sliding my hands from his knees up his thighs, I leaned into him.

"Gotcha."

I didn't say another word, reaching toward his waist and quickly undoing the belt and unfastening his pants. Although I was eager to see his dick, a thick cloud of failure hovered over me, making my hands tremble as I reached inside of his pants and pulled him free. As soon as I laid eyes on him, I sucked in a breath. Rhone was a big boy and he had the dick to match. I recalled the picture he'd sent me when I inquired about his size. My eyes shot to one of his hands, which were both resting along the top of the two-seat sofa, before flicking to his face to find the barest hint of a smirk playing at the corner of his lips. He knew what he was working with, and the confidence in that look made the tingle that was in my shoulders when I walked in, travel down to settle between my thighs.

After rolling on the condom, I grasped him with both hands before licking my lips and taking him into my mouth. The length gave me enough room to circle him in my hands, but the girth made it a tight fit. My lips were stretched wide, but not uncomfortably, so I figured I could reasonably manage to swallow at least half of him down, but for some reason, my lips just wouldn't slide down further. Since I couldn't move my mouth beyond his tip, I began pumping him with my hands.

Squeezing him tightly, I quickly moved up and down as if he were a Shake Weight. His thighs jerked beneath my elbows, and I brought my eyes to his face expecting to find his face contorted in pleasure. Instead, his eyes were wide with alarm, and his lips were balled into his mouth.

Panic seized me, and I began rolling my lips, attempting to massage him, trying to give the little bit of him that I had in my mouth pleasure along with his shaft.

"Ah, shit!"

His was trembling beneath me, and I had a tiny sliver of hope that it was because he was about to cum, but then his hands closed over mine and peeled my fingers off of him and the illusion shattered. I let him fall from my lips and he instantly cradled his softened dick with both hands, his head back against the sofa as his chest heaved. He looked utterly relieved to be free of me, and that was it. That was the final straw that broke the remnants of my pride.

Immediately, a sob burst forth from my mouth and I hurriedly slapped my hands over my lips to capture the sound. Rhone's head popped up from the sofa and he stared at me, regret shining brightly in his deep brown eyes. I couldn't take that. If it wasn't bad enough to have a man I'd once loved throw my failure in my face, now a virtual stranger who'd had the benefit of knowing what to expect beforehand *regretted* giving me a chance. Scrambling to my feet, I rushed across the room, heading for the bathroom.

"Malina, wait!"

Just as my hands gripped the doorknob, I turned to see Rhone on his feet, tucking his flaccid dick back into his pants. He started for me and I quickly pulled open the door and rushed inside, finding myself not in the bathroom, but a square, walk-in-closet closet. *Fuck my life.* With my back in one corner, I slid down the wall and buried my face in my hands, trying and failing to hold back tears.

The crying only made me more upset, because I wasn't even sad—I was angry as hell and embarrassed beyond imagination. Before I could wallow too deeply, the door cracked open and Rhone appeared in the doorway. I could feel his stare, but I refused to look at him, not needing to see the disappointment on his face to know it was there. I expected him to shut the door, or ask me to come out so that we could talk, but he once again surprised me by entering the closet and squeezing his big body into the corner opposite me. Then he reached across the small space and wrapped a hand around my calf.

"I'm sorry."

Shocked, I lifted my head and swung my eyes to his face.

"What are you apologizing for? Your only job was to provide dick and you went above and beyond by bringing an eggplant."

His lips twitched, and I couldn't help but eye his mouth wistfully. Maybe if I hadn't been so damn awful he would've rewarded me with a kiss. Shaking my head, I dropped my gaze back to my lap.

"I should be the only one apologizing. In fact," I faced him again, meeting those brown irises that held kindness and compassion, "I apologize, Rhone. You were apparently in pain and I was oblivious. You—and your dick—deserve better."

He shook his head. "It's alright. You gave me a heads up beforehand. I knew what to expect."

A morose sigh escaped my lips, and my shoulders sagged. "It's not alright. I could have broken something!"

An amused laugh filled the small space, the low rumble curling around my head and making funny things happen in the pit of my belly.

"I can guarantee that I wouldn't have let you break anything. Besides, I told you to show me what you got and that's what you did."

"I showed you what I *don't got*," I muttered darkly.

Rhone squeezed my calf, making my nipples tighten beneath my blouse. Blinking rapidly, I glanced down at his big hand on me before trailing my eyes up to his face. He wore a small smile, not the disappointment I deserved, and an answering smile appeared on my face.

"There you go," he murmured, going from

squeezing to gently rubbing up and down. "Now that we've gotten this first session out of the way, I know what we need to work on for next time."

Peeling my eyes from his hand on me, I looked up in confusion, not quite believing that he was saying what it sounded like he was saying.

"Next time?"

He nodded, continuously rubbing my calf. "Yes. You said you wanted to learn how to suck dick, right?" He paused, clearly waiting for me to respond, and I nodded quickly. "I'm going to teach you, but it won't happen in an hour. It takes time. Practice."

"Practice?" I repeated, feeling a little lightheaded both from the way he was touching me and the words coming out of his mouth.

Grinning, he squeezed me again. "Haven't you ever heard the phrase *practice makes perfect*?"

I nodded lamely. Of course, I had. I just never thought I'd be applying it to fellatio.

"Good. Then you should understand that we're going to practice this thing until your technique is perfect."

"You'll still help me?"

"Hell yeah! Now that I've seen what you're working with, I'd feel like the biggest asshole on the planet—behind your piece-of-shit ex—if I let you go out like that. All offense to that dude intended."

I cringed, not because he'd insulted Blaine, but because I'd done so poorly that Rhone felt a sense of duty to help me. His reaction was the most embarrassing thing I'd ever experienced.

"Okay," I said with a nod. "Let's do this."

FOUR

SYLLABUS

"What the hell is this?" I could admit that my voice was a little shrill, but I felt knocked off balance.

"It's your lesson plan," Rhone replied smoothly, his attention never leaving my face.

"Lesson plan?" I repeated blankly, my eyes roving the paper in my hands.

It wasn't clicking for me. It had been a week since my failed attempt at a blow job, and we were meeting for a second go-round. The moment that I'd walked through the door, Rhone surprised me by looping an arm around my waist and wrapping me in a tight hug. I was immediately enveloped in his scent—his warmth—and his body felt so good against mine that I almost whimpered in protest when he pulled away entirely too soon. He was more dressed down today than the first time we'd met, but still not quite casual. He wore dark-wash jeans and another button-down.

Closing the door behind me, Rhone quickly herded me across the room to sit in the wingback chair, and then handed me a sheet of paper before sitting in the center of the sofa. I stared down at the paper, rife with confusion, as the bold heading jumped out at me.

Knob-Slobbing Lessons

Face heating, I sucked in a breath and looked at Rhone.

His head bobbed. "Yes. You want to learn and, now that I've seen your skill level, we can focus on the areas you need improvement."

"Wait," I sat forward in the chair and squinted at him. "Why are you saying that like the whole thing wasn't bad?"

His eyes were full of kindness as he returned my gaze. "The entire experience wasn't unpleasant, Malina. The actual act of you sucking my dick wasn't...ideal...but that isn't the entirety of what makes oral enjoyable. Don't get me wrong; it's impor-tant, but not the sole entity of importance." He nodded to the paper in my hand and picked up an identical one from the low table that was back in its rightful position. "Now, shall we get to it?"

With wide eyes, I nodded and sat back in the chair, lifting the paper closer to my face to read along as he read it out loud.

"There are five areas we need to cover that I believe will net you your desired result. Those areas are ambiance, location, lubrication, technique, and culmination." He looked up at me, peering over the rims of his glasses in a way that was oddly sexy as hell. "You with me so far?"

"Mmhm," I assured him with a quick nod. The information on the page was…a lot, but listening to Rhone's smooth voice read it to me made everything seem less awkward.

"Good," he murmured, turning his attention back to the paper. "Ambiance is made up of many things. It's what you might call the vibe, and it's more than just the music playing in the background—if you even decide to have music." Again he looked at me. "How you feel is important, Malina. You have to want to do it; if you don't, the act becomes tedious and unpleasant for both parties. You should feel sexy; this is about you as much as it is about your partner. Style your hair in a way that you love, and put on clothes that make you blow yourself kisses in the mirror. If you're wearing constricting or stuffy clothing, then that's going to affect how you feel, and subsequently, the performance you give. Lastly, you absolutely need to feel in control. All of those factors determine the quality of the head you're giving."

My brows furrowed. "How can I possibly feel in control when I'm literally on my knees?"

Rhone's thick lips curved into a grin, and I clutched my paper tightly in my hand, overcome with the desire to kiss him.

"Your physical position doesn't determine whether or not you're in control. While performing oral can be an act of submission, it is not in itself a submissive act. The person giving head is, without a doubt, the one in control. You set the pace; you chose the pressure; you have the final say when your partner comes. The control is yours and yours alone. When you lean into that control—that power—your partner is at your mercy. Remember that."

He winked at me, and my cheeks heated. I was hot and bothered just from listening to him talk about the act, and we were only on the first bullet-point. How the hell was I supposed to make it through four more of these?

"Next is location. It isn't just about whether you do it in the backseat of your car or the living room;

it's also about positioning and how that affects your ability."

Licking my lips, I stared down at the paper. "Okay, I'll bite. What do you mean by positioning?"

"When I say positioning, I mean of bodies. There is a difference from giving head when your partner is standing up, leaning against the front door, and sitting on the sofa, or lying in bed. Each of these positions requires different muscles to be used and allows you to perform in multiple ways. It's something to consider when weighing your stamina against what you're trying to achieve."

I frowned once more, confused yet again. "Isn't the purpose of sucking dick to get the other person to cum?"

Rhone lifted a hand into the air and rocked it back and forth. "More or less. Sometimes it can be about more than simply cumming. Maybe you and your partner are experimenting with edging, and you're in it for the long haul. That probably wouldn't be the best time to be on your knees unless you have kneepads or a special cushion. Conversely, maybe you want to reward your partner at the end of the day with a gentle nightcap of an orgasm. Something quick and sweet."

My hand fluttered up to my neck, and I tugged on the neckline of my blouse. It was so much to take in, and I was grateful that Rhone was taking the time to give me a genuine education about this. A flare of anger rose inside of me when I thought about how I could have been learning these things over time if Blaine had chosen to just—

No.

Shaking my head, I cleared all thoughts of the man who might as well had already been my ex several months before we'd officially split from my mind. I was here with Rhone, and he was putting in more effort than anyone before him. For that reason alone, he deserved 150% of my attention. Licking my lips, I cut my eyes over to my oral educator, a slick grin on my face.

"I think I know what lubrication is. We can skip that one."

He smirked. "I'll keep this one brief then. The bottom line is that you *always* need lubrication. Whether you use a water-based lubricant or an *abundance* of saliva."

The emphasis he put on the word abundance made me groan as I thought back to the previous week. Despite how bad I was at giving head, I knew better than to only lick my lips before going down. I could only attribute my misstep to my nerves, which brought me back to Rhone's first point—ambiance. If I had been comfortable about the act leading up to my arrival, then at the very least, I would have brought a packet of flavored lube with me. Properly chastened, even though he hadn't uttered a word of admonishment, I nodded.

"Gotcha."

With an answering nod, Rhone offered me a smile before returning to the final two areas.

"Let's talk technique. There are some basics, like no teeth, but every person is different so, this is something you have to learn by doing *and* discussing with your partner. The standard, which is a great fall back, is the simple bob. It's a classic that gets the job done. There is also the combination of the bob and a hand job which can be effective *only* if there is proper lubrication and the pressure is right."

"Oh my God," I mumbled, covering my face with my hand. Everything I'd done that first night had been basic-level fuck-ups.

"Hey." Rhone's voice was gentle as he tried to get my attention. I looked up, face scrunched in mortification. "Let that shit go, Malina," he commanded, somehow managing to sound firm while still being kind. "It happened, and now we're moving forward. You're going to learn what to do, and when you know, everything before now will be a funny memory that you'll tell your girlfriends. Okay?"

I stared at him for a moment, wondering why I

hadn't met him in a different capacity. The amount of patience and grace he'd extended to me in the two days that I'd spent with him made me want to know him better. Quita would tell me that everything happened for a reason, but outside of learning how to suck some future, faceless man's dick, I couldn't yet see the purpose in meeting a man who intrigued me and aroused me just by speaking. There was a soothing quality to his voice that made it easy to believe him when he said that everything would work out.

Sighing, I nodded. "Okay." There was nothing to gain from wracking my brain about it.

Rhone dipped his chin twice and held up the paper. "Another thing about technique is paying attention to your partner. They will always give you cues to let you know how you're doing. They could be verbal or nonverbal. Sometimes they might speak, but not everyone is a talker. Moans, groans, grunts, whimpers; all of those are verbal. Lip biting, legs shaking, heavy breathing, fists clenching; those are nonverbal cues. Also, pay attention to facial expressions. Those generally don't lie."

Nodding, I thought back to the look in his eyes a week earlier and was overcome with shame. That man had genuine worry in his eyes and all I did was jerk his dick harder. With his eyes back on the paper,

Rhone didn't notice my silence as I was lost in thought. He continued.

"Last but not least, the culmination. This is what everything you've been doing manifests as. The pot of gold at the end of the rainbow."

Snatched out of my thoughts, I blinked and peered over at him. "The cumming?"

A smirk played at his lips. "The cumming. You have to decide what you want to do when your partner climaxes. If you're using condoms, obviously that's the first option, but if you're with someone you trust and those aren't being used?" He shrugged. "Well, then you have to decide if you will spit or swallow. If neither of those is an option, then you have to consider clean-up methods. Do you have a specific place you want it to land? Your face or breasts, perhaps? Or would you rather just let it fly and wipe up the mess later? It's all something to consider beforehand so that you can focus on your performance during the act."

Spit or swallow. Facials.

Just thinking about all of it had me hotter than a fire in July. Obviously, I wasn't going to get everything right on the first go-round after this "lesson plan", but now I was eager to try, and it wasn't just for some sort of revenge. I wanted to see if I could be the one in control and if I could make Rhone lose the hold he had on his.

"Now," he began, and my chest heaved in anticipation as I watched him set his sheet of paper on the table before leaning back against the sofa, his arms draped along the back, "are you ready to practice?"

FIVE

MID-TERMS

R hone hadn't been kidding that first night when he said he was going to teach me. We'd spent the rest of that second night, and all of the third, going over the "lesson plan" line-by-line. Rhone had figuratively held my hand as he coached me through each phase, encouraging me, pushing me, and never putting me down, despite my missteps. Through three nights of my face in his lap, I'd made strides, but I still hadn't been able to make him cum.

Graciously, he'd insisted that it wasn't a big deal, reminding me that I was learning and that it was more important to master the first four areas before worrying about the lack of…finishing. Everything he'd said made sense, but I was ready for the finale. I was done with failing and was now bound and determined to execute each area of the perfect blow job, including reaching the culmination stage. I was beyond ready to figure out what to do with his cum. I hadn't told Rhone, but I desperately wanted to taste it. I wanted his cum on my tongue, and I wouldn't consider these lessons a success until I experienced that.

We'd reached the fourth lesson in this however-long journey, and as I stood on the other side of the door, waiting to be invited inside, the butterflies in my stomach were from a different set of nerves. At the end of lesson three, I'd expressed my frustration with the location portion of these lessons. Constantly meeting at a hotel overshadowed the comfort I felt around Rhone, making the entire experience feel... impersonal. How could I feel relaxed and in control when I wasn't in a relaxed environment? And because Rhone was Rhone—a thoughtful and compassionate person—he gave me the option of continuing our lessons at his house. I agreed to it, thinking that the change in environment would be beneficial for him as well. Maybe the familiar surroundings would allow him to relax enough to let the chopper spray.

When Rhone opened the door, I could already see the evidence of how the location change was working. Unlike every other time that we'd met up, he was dressed casually for once. Clad in black jogging pants and a Franklin University alumni tee, he somehow managed to be even sexier than when he was buttoned up—which was saying a lot. Smiling, he eyed me from head-to-toe as he stepped back to let me in.

"Glad you found it okay," he murmured as I slipped past him and entered the foyer.

I was pretty sure his eyes were on my ass. It was the night before Christmas Eve, but still seventy degrees outside, which meant I could still have my legs out. Forgoing my usual skirt and stockings combination, I'd opted for a silver slip-dress that fell to mid-thigh, and gray, low-top Chucks. I had a mission in mind, and comfort was the name of the game.

"Would you like a tour?"

Glancing over my shoulder, I felt a thrill zip through me at the open desire on Rhone's face. Every time he looked at me, it was evident that he wanted to do more than let me put my mouth on him, and every time I caught his gape, I was tempted to let him. Smirking, I waited for his eyes to lift from my ass to my face. There was no shame to be found.

"Where's the couch?" I asked pointedly.

Catching my drift, he grinned. "Right through here."

He led me into the living room, and my attention

was immediately stolen by the stuffed bookshelves that bracketed the ginormous flat screen mounted on the wall. Without even realizing it, my course changed, and I found myself standing in front of the bookshelf closest to the entrance. The titles jumped out at me, and my grin stretched wide when I noticed some of my favorites. Picking up one well-worn Zora Neale Hurston tome, I began flipping through it, shocked and impressed by the notes scribbled in the margins and the many arrow-shaped sticky notes used as placeholders.

More curious than ever about the man who had become my tutor, I peeked over my shoulder at him. He was sitting in the center of the sofa, just as he did at the hotel, but instead of a corduroy settee, the leather sectional looked long—and deep—enough for Rhone to lie down comfortably. As expected, his eyes were on me, but I'd been prepared to find him wearing an amused mien, not the intense gape of a man prepared to completely release the reins of control into my hands.

By sheer nature of his size, Rhone commanded respect, and even the glasses he wore didn't detract from that. Paradoxically, with something as superficial as tutoring me on the art of giving head, he possessed an air of authority and importance that seemed as intrinsic to his being as the smooth sepia tone of his skin. Having a man like that ready and willing to be at my mercy was like downing a shot of top-shelf tequila, followed by a hit of the most eclectic strain of weed. The high it triggered was buzzing beneath my skin, and my intuition told me that tonight, I would finally achieve the success I had been chasing. Unlike the previous times that Rhone and I had met, a sense of calm came over me. I was Superhead, and I was about to pull a rabbit out of a hat with my mouth.

I replaced the book, taking care not to bend the cover or disturb the abundance of notes as I slid it back among the Baldwins and Morrisons. Wordlessly, I padded toward him, sinking to my knees atop the over-sized cushion that he'd already placed between his feet. Rubbing up and down his thighs, I met his gaze.

"Pull it out."

He did as I commanded, first raising his hips a few inches and pushing his pants down, then reaching into his waistband to unearth the hardened erection I was there for. There were no questions, nor raised brows, and I figured that maybe he realized how this night was supposed to go just as I did. I licked my palm and gripped him at the base before sliding my hand up to the tip, slowly increasing the pressure as I did so.

His regard didn't stray from my face, but he elicited a soft grunt that let me know he wasn't unaffected. *Good.* I dove in, taking him into my mouth and running my tongue along the underside of his rigid length, doing the double duty of creating more saliva and widening my mouth so more of him could fit.

"Careful," he warned in a low voice, eliciting a glare from me.

I pulled off of his dick with an audible pop. "No talking, remember?" I reminded him. A week earlier, after our third night of lessons, Rhone informed me that tonight would be something like a test.

"Closed book," he'd added after I'd given him a wide-eyed look.

"What does that mean?"

"It means I won't be giving you any guidance. I'm going to sit back and let you do your thing.

A small part of me had been nervous, but a larger part had been excited to finally get a chance to put in work. I couldn't do my thing if Rhone didn't trust me to at least do a decent job.

Rhone shook his head. "You want me to talk. You want me to—"

"I want you to shut the fuck up unless you're screaming for mercy," I snapped, annoyed that he was throwing off my flow. "Save the tips and warnings for another day. Unless you're usually vocal, I don't want to hear a word out of your mouth, and since you have yet to show yourself a talker, hush!"

He quirked a brow—respect shining in his eyes—and nodded. Like a sexy cornball, he mimed zipping his lips closed and leaned back to rest his hands along the back of the couch. Shaking my head softly, I pursed my lips and thought about his interrupted warning. *Where had I gone wrong so quickly?* Oh. Maybe I was going *too* quickly, and that was the point.

Watching porn might have you thinking that you need to jump in there full throttle, and that's fine if you know what you're doing. For a beginner, all you need to know is that slow and steady, cum will make.

Slow and steady. I could do that. Rolling my shoulders back, I leaned forward and dribbled onto his dick. I could feel the weight of his gaze on me, but I refused to look up, focusing on the task at hand. Taking his lubricated dick between my palms, I massaged him from base to tip, alternating between increasing and decreasing the pressure with every repetition. Rhone's grunts and groans started up, and grew lengthier as I put my shoulders into it, but his hands had yet to so much as twitch.

Innocuous as it were, I considered it a personal challenge to get his hands off of the back of that couch. Thanks to the work I'd put in with my hands, a clear drop of precum formed on his tip. With that as my green light, I bent forward and took him into my mouth. At first, just the tip. Flicking my tongue against the pearlescent drop, I pursed my lips to kiss the slit and then opened my mouth to gradually swallow him down. I hit as far as I could go, stopping just before the need to gag arose, and then retreating just as slowly, only to repeat the motion a few more times.

With drool pouring down my chin, I continued pumping him as I went, twisting my neck back and forth as I swallowed him down over and over. As the minutes flew by, I felt my body respond to the way Rhone was reacting, increasingly turned on by his noises coming out of his mouth and the way his body was twitching. When his hands came from the back of the couch and clasped on top of his head, I did an internal cheer and increased my suction.

"Oh shit," he grumbled. "*Fuck!*"

Pay attention to my voice. You can tell how I like it with my words and my inflections.

His voice was a little strained, and I wanted to pat myself on the back for making that happen. Instead, I dropped one hand between my legs and wrapped the other around the base of his shaft, steadily jacking him as I slipped my fingers past the elastic edge of my panties and dragged them through my wetness. Moaning, I bobbed my head, twisting back and forth with every descent. When I felt his hand at the back of my head, gripping my ponytail fiercely, I knew that he was close.

"Malina, *goddamn*," he nearly whined. "Suck this fucking dick, baby."

Fueled by the desperation in his voice, I increased my speed and hollowed my cheeks. Between my legs, I slid two fingers into my pussy and pumped vigorously. I was so damn turned on that it wouldn't take much to get me off, and I could tell that Rhone was nearly there as well.

Spit or swallow? What's it gonna be?

"I'm 'bout to come!" he moaned.

With that announcement, I went in for the kill, taking him as deep into my throat as he could go— until I gagged and had to retreat. Between my legs, I thumbed my clit in rapid, faltering strokes until I issued a muffled cry as I came. I couldn't stop until I'd finished my mission, repeatedly descending on his dick to bring him to the edge and push him over. The hand not holding my hair caressed my cheek softly, and then Rhone slipped a thumb into the corner of my mouth. I flicked my tongue over against the tip of his finger before I went in for a second attempt to deep-throat him, almost touching the curls at the base before I gagged again.

It wasn't a failure though.

"*Fuuuuck!*"

Rhone dropped his head back against the couch as his dick pulsed between my lips and he shot his release at the back of my throat. But I couldn't taste it, which had been number one on my wishlist, so I slowly eased up, continually jacking him as I ascended, until I felt a spurt of his cum splash across the back of my tongue. I swallowed down the salty fluid and continued jacking him until he began to soften in my hands. Once he was completely drained, I sat back on my haunches and grinned at the way his chest was heaving. His eyelids were so low that he almost looked asleep, but I knew in the way that my body was taut with awareness, that he was staring at me.

"So," I quipped hoarsely, "how'd I do?"

SIX

FINALS

Anticipation buzzed along my veins. The high from making Rhone cum with my mouth was unmatched. The look on his face, the way his eyes had tightened, brows furrowed, the guttural groan that had slipped past his lips. It had all been on my mind for three days straight.

I needed it.

Making it happen again was all that I'd been able to think about, which is why I was sitting outside of Rhone's house waiting for him to answer his phone. This was reckless. It wasn't how things were done between us, but I couldn't *not* be here. I craved him; needed his scent on my upper lip and his taste on my tongue.

"Hello?" Rhone greeted when he finally answered the phone after three rings.

"I'm ready for my next lesson."

He chuckled, the rumbling sound wrapping around me in the quiet cabin of my car and traveling down my spine to settle in the pit of my stomach.

"You know damn well that you're a pro now. After last time, I can't imagine what else I could teach you."

I shook my head, although he couldn't see me. "It doesn't work like that. After three failures, one win doesn't make me fixed."

The line went silent for a moment before Rhone quietly proclaimed, "You were never broken, Malina." His tone was low but full of authority, turning me on something fierce.

"I want you," I whispered, finally coming out and saying the thing I'd been avoiding acknowledging. I could hear the hitch in his breath.

"What are you trying to say? You want *me*...or you want this dick? Because I didn't think you were interested in the former."

Releasing a breath through my nose, I licked my lips. One of the many non-sexual things I'd learned about Rhone since meeting him, was that he wasn't going to let me get away with hinting at anything. He forced me to make declarations with my chest and stand up in them.

"You, Rhone. I want you. Dick is abundant, but there's only one Rhone Givens."

"Shit, Malina," he muttered gruffly, "when you comin'?"

Shutting off my car, I pushed open my door and quickly stepped out of my car. "Right now. Come to the door."

I hung up the phone and slid it into my purse as I started up the walkway. The front door opened before I reached it, revealing Rhone standing there in a pair of mesh athletic shorts and a Franklin tee with the sleeves cut off. The closer I got to him, the hotter I became until I stood before him, *smoldering* with liquid desire coursing through my veins.

He let me inside, devouring me with his eyes, displaying his every emotion right there on his face for me to see. Rhone wanted me equally as much as I wanted him, but there was some skepticism there as well. I understood it, because of how we'd met—*why* we'd met—but I didn't know how to reassure him. Hell, I couldn't even explain it in my mind, I just knew that I wanted him, and since he also wanted me, as soon as he closed that door, he was going to get me.

Once he closed the door, after I crossed the threshold of his home, it was as if a starting pistol had been shot. I lunged for him just as he started toward me, and he caught me in his arms, frantically meeting my mouth with his own as he pulled my legs around his waist, palming my ass with his large hands. He walked us further into the house, massaging my cheeks through the thin fabric of my leggings, and I kissed him with a fervency that I couldn't explain. To my favor, it seemed there was no explanation needed, and Rhone returned my energy a hundred-fold with an urgency that made several different parts of me thump and pulse.

It didn't make sense. It seemed like only days had passed since I'd woken up next to Blaine, and yet it also felt as if every fiber of my being had always desired Rhone. He was under my skin, and even that didn't seem close enough. Suddenly, Rhone was bending at the waist, and I opened my eyes to realize that we were in his bedroom, and he was placing me in his king-size bed. Reaching down, he tugged my black Chucks off of my feet before stepping back and pulling his shirt over his head.

While he undressed, I quickly shimmied out of my leggings and hoodie, tossing them and my panties onto the floor. Naked, I kept my eyes on Rhone as I scooted backward into the center of the bed. The appreciation on his face was ego-boosting, and it hit me that this was the first time he'd seen me —all of me. He joined me on the bed, and I moved to reach for his dick, but he clocked my intent and grabbed my hands to stop me.

"I might not have been the student, but can I have an opportunity to showcase my knowledge?"

I started to ask what he meant, but then it hit me like a ton of bricks, and my chest heaved in surprise. *Oh.* Well, I would never deny a hungry man a good meal, so I nodded and sat my ass down on the soft duvet, leaning back on my elbows as Rhone laid on his belly and spread my legs wide. With bated breath, I watched him nuzzle the dark curls on my mound before tracing the already damp lips of my pussy with his nose.

"You smell so fucking good," he murmured against me.

I started to thank him, but the acknowledgment died in my throat when he dove tongue-first into my pussy.

"Oh God," I wailed, exhaling sharply as he licked and slurped and *devoured* me.

Rhone put his entire face in my pussy, one a mission to get to the center of the Tootsie pop located between my legs. When he sucked my clit into his mouth and simultaneously flicked his tongue back and forth against it, I clutched at the sheets, back bowed, and screamed at the top of my lungs. My climax seemed ongoing, with wave after wave of pleasure crashing into my body until I was a trembling husk of boneless flesh. As tremors wracked my body, Rhone wiped his mouth with the back of his hand, and came onto his knees, staring down at me with an unreadable expression on his face.

"You still want me?"

With great effort, I cracked my eyelids open and peered up at him, noting the hint of vulnerability beneath the layer of unbridled yearning. Breathing heavily, I nodded.

"More than ever," I replied, spreading my legs even further to make room for his big body to settle between them.

Scooting closer, he lifted one of my legs over his hip as he leaned down to kiss me hungrily. I wrapped my arms around his neck, pressing up into the kiss, relishing the taste of me on his tongue, loving the feel of his plush lips on mine. And as I lost myself in his mouth, I felt him guide his dick into my opening, breaching my soaked folds with little to no resistance. Sucking in a breath at the intrusion, I broke our kiss to push my head back into the mattress as he pushed his hips forward, filling me up inch-by-inch. He dropped his head, peppering kisses along the column of my neck and across my shoulder as he moved inside of me.

The patience that I'd seen Rhone exhibit while

teaching me how to please him with my mouth was front and center while he was inside me. Our coupling was neither hurried nor fleeting. He rocked into me deliberately, taking his time, drawing out the moment until my body was buzzing with sensation. Every brush of his skin against my own felt like a jolt of electricity, overwhelming me until I cried out for release, and gentleman that he was, Rhone answered my plea. Moving back onto his knees, he straddled one of my legs and twisted my hips so that I was on my side. After lifting my other leg into the air, he stroked me deeper than ever, but at that same leisurely pace.

The angle he'd chosen put his dick on a direct course to my g-spot, and it only took a handful of thrusts for me to grip handfuls of my locs and tug while I moaned through a second orgasm. The uncontrollable spasming of my pussy as I came triggered his release. His groan tapered into a whimper, and he gripped my thighs tightly as his movements stuttered. When his dick stopped twitching inside of me, he pulled out and fell onto the bed, positioning most of his weight on the bed as he laid his head on my stomach.

Feeling content and utterly sated, I scraped my fingers against his scalp, allowing my body time to come down from the high he'd put me on. Unfortunately, the peaceful moment we were sharing came to a screeching halt when I felt the evidence of our raw sex begin its descent out of my body. Carefully, so as not to activate my pelvic muscles, I knocked my thighs against his shoulders.

"Rhone, get up. I need to go to the bathroom."

Immediately, he began to rise, only to stop and peer down at me curiously. I bucked my eyes at him, wondering why he wasn't moving off of me.

"Do you need to pee?" he asked, almost conversationally.

My brows knitted as I frowned. "Isn't that what most people do in the bathroom?"

"I know what most people do; I'm asking if that's what *you* need to do."

The question was bizarre but considering that I'd been regularly sucking his dick for the last four weeks, there was no need to harbor modesty for anything. Huffing a breath, I met his gaze.

"You came in me, Rhone. I need to push that shit out."

He nodded as if that was the answer he'd been expecting, and I sighed in relief when he lifted off of me. But instead of moving completely so that I could sit up or scoot from under him, he grabbed the backs of my thighs and pulled me closer.

"Push it out."

Blinking rapidly, I stared at him, but his eyes were on my exposed center, waiting.

"I—" The protest formed on my lips, but then I swallowed it down.

How different was this from any of the other wildly intimate things we'd done? I mean, I'd just let the man raw me our first time having sex, and I'd swallowed his cum a few days earlier. It didn't matter that we'd exchanged status information before we met up that first time, or that I was three years into a five year IUD. Sucking my lower lip into my mouth, I nibbled on it and studied his face as I engaged my pelvic muscles and bored down.

It was easy to pinpoint the exact moment that his essence visibly seeped out of me. His nostrils flared, eyes darkened, and he bent to press a kiss to my inner thigh. When he lifted his eyes to my face, the fire in those dark brown depths made goosebumps erupt all over my skin. Without him saying a word, I realized at that moment that I wasn't likely to leave his home that night. I'd yet to have his taste on my tongue, but beyond that, the look in his eyes made it unequivocally understood that *he* wasn't done with *me*.

SEVEN

GRADUATION

New Year's Eve arrived and I found myself back at Quita and Simon's sprawling home, feeling conflicted. It had only been a few days since I'd seen Rhone—since I'd fucked Rhone—but I wished that I had asked him to come with me that evening. It was a wild thought because outside of me semi-regularly slobbing on his knob, we hadn't spent any time together.

"Girl, why are you standing over here by the food like a lonely bitch?"

I was yanked out of my thoughts by Quita walking up to me and sliding an arm around my waist. She eyed me curiously as I shook my head.

"Quita, I'm buggin'."

Her eyebrows knitted. "What's up?"

Peeking around her to see if anyone was hovering

near the dining room, I quickly explained my dilemma. She already knew all about Rhone and our "lessons", but I hadn't had a chance to tell her about our latest…escapade. I finished the story and waited for her response.

"Oh no!" she gasped, startling me.

"What?" I asked her, eyes wide with concern. "What is it?"

"You got on your knees to suck his dick, but he picked you up and then knocked you down."

Covering my face, I groaned. She was so damn extra. "Quita, please go away. Nobody has time for you to be randomly dropping Keri Hilson lyrics into perfectly sane conversations."

Amused, she cackled. "Why? Because you decided to open your legs instead of your mouth, and now you're sprung?"

With wide eyes, I looked around, wondering who the hell she was talking about. "*Who's sprung?*" I demanded incredulously. "Surely not I!"

"You, indeed," she insisted, wearing an amused grin so wide it looked like her cheeks would split across her face like the Joker. "You got caught up by the penile pedagogue, and now you're hot for teacher."

"The what and what?!" I screeched, trying not to burst into laughter. I didn't want to encourage her but my chest was already throbbing from trying to hold the air in.

"The siphon sophist. The guzzling governor. The sloppy toppy tutor."

Shaking my head, I took a step away from her. "Simon!" I yelled, signaling for immediate backup. A few heads peeked into the dining room, likely trying to see what the hell was going on, but I ignored them. "Simon!"

I was gearing up to scream for Quita's husband a third time when the man in question entered the dining room through the kitchen and immediately stepped up behind Quita, who was doubled-over with laughter. Wrapping his arms around his wife, he dropped a kiss on her temple before looking at me.

"I'm here, woman," he declared, a good-natured smile on his face despite the grumbling tone he'd used. "Where's the goddamn fire?"

I pointed at Quita, who hadn't stopped giggling. "Your wife is in here being a menace. Please get her."

He looked back and forth between the two of us before fixing his gaze on Quita.

"What'd you do?"

It took her a moment to catch her breath, and then she shook her head. "I'm just teasing her about—"

"Quita," I warned. She was not allowed to tell my business, even to her husband.

Quita rolled her eyes playfully before she and Simon shared a look.

"You know what?" Simon began after a moment, turning his gaze back on me. "Come with me, Malina. I want to officially introduce you to someone."

With furrowed brows, I stared at the two of them, not missing how Quita elbowed him in the ribs before aiming a censoring glare at the side of his face.

"Okay..." I drawled, then turned to refill my champagne flute. Once that was done, I narrowed my eyes and shot Quita a glare before following Simon into the living room.

He led me to a corner of the bright and open space, where some of his colleagues were deep in discussion. I recognized a few of the people from when I would attend events with Blaine, and reflexively cast a searching glance around. I'd only arrived half an hour ago and hadn't yet seen him, but I was sure Blaine was lurking somewhere in the house. He and Simon had been friends for years, and even though he'd missed Friendsgiving, he wouldn't dare skip out on the annual New Year's Eve party. We reached the group, and Simon dropped a hand onto the shoulder of a man whose back was to us. He turned around, and my stomach lurched in surprise once I saw his face.

It was Rhone!

His brows rose when those deep brown eyes that I quite enjoyed looked up and met mine, but the lack of surprise on his face was evident. My brows knitted momentarily. *What the hell?* Had he already known who I was?

"Forgive the interruption, Rhone," Simon began, his hand still on Rhone's shoulder, "but I have someone that I want to introduce you to. This is Malina; the woman I mentioned to you." Turning to me, Simon added, "Malina, this is Rhone. He's one of the professors in my department."

Shocked, my lips parted, and my eyes were wide as my gaze bounced back and forth between the two men. Simon was dean over the African American studies department at Franklin. If Rhone taught in his department, then there was also a probability that he knew Blaine. Swinging my head toward Simon, I shook my head as if to clear away cobwebs. "Hold on a second. Did you just say that you *mentioned* me?"

Simon grinned widely, unperturbed by the aghast expression I wore. "Yep. Go ahead and talk amongst yourselves," he leaned into my ear and added, "since you know each other already anyway."

My jaw dropped toward the floor as I watched Simon squeeze Rhone's shoulder before winking at me and walking off. Silently, I stood rooted to the spot while his lanky frame practically skipped out of the living room, certain he was headed for his motor-mouth wife, who was probably standing on the other side of the wall, waiting for an update. It was confirmed. Quita was definitely a traitor. Simon's little introduction proved that Quita had not only told him about my lessons, but had told him *who* I'd been "studying" with.

Finally, I turned back to Rhone to see him gaping at me with hooded eyes.

"Always so damn beautiful," he murmured as he trailed his gaze up my body.

A flush of heat crept across my face as he took in my black and gold, glittery mini-dress, and I dropped my eyes to the drink in my hand.

"Thank you. You look good enough to eat your-self." And he did. He was sexy in the black sweater and tan slacks he wore.

"Come on," he instructed, palming my elbow and guiding me away from the group he'd been conversing with. We were only a few feet away when he moved closer to me, stepping into the circle of my personal space, brushing my arm with his chest and belly. I could feel his body heat as he brought his lips to my ear.

"I'm happy to see you." His warm breath brushed over my ear, eliciting a shiver, as his words brought a pleased smile to my face.

Canting my head slightly, I glanced at him from the corner of my eye, and sipped from my glass. "Yeah?"

"Yeah," he assured me, nodding to solidify it.

Something like relief mixed with the pleasure I felt, bringing a soft smile to my lips. "I'm happy to see you, too."

Reaching up, he brushed a few of my locs off of my shoulder, barely caressing my neck with the pads of his fingertips. The feather-lite touch made a shiver run through me, and I pushed out a steadying breath. He leaned into me again, and then I held my breath so that I could hear him over the pounding of my heart.

"You could call me, you know. You don't have to wait for a lesson."

I let my eyes flutter closed, a soft smile on my lips as I reminded him, "I didn't wait the last time."

"*Malina*," he murmured in an agonized tone that I didn't recognize but was no less affected by.

Turning my head toward him, I opened my eyes, and my breath halted in my throat. It didn't matter that we were in a room full of people, some of which were his colleagues. Rhone clearly saw nothing and no one but me. His eyes were dark with a primal desire that I knew carnally and wanted to know again, right that moment. The knowledge that I had his full attention was heady; intoxicating. It was similar to the way I'd felt that last night we'd spent together, when we'd met eyes just before he came, spilling his seed down my throat while my lips were stretched around his dick.

"Hey there, Malina."

Startled, I blinked rapidly to clear away the cocoon of lust that Rhone and I had found ourselves in. I'd been too lost in the swirl of Rhone's eyes to notice that Blaine had walked up to us. Turning to him, I took him in. With one hand holding a drink and the other shoved into the pocket of his corduroys, he appeared cool and collected on the surface, but his face told a different story. He wore a friendly smile, but his usually warm, brown eyes were narrowed and bouncing suspiciously from me to Rhone.

"Oh, hello, Blaine."

Blaine barely acknowledged my greeting before turning to Rhone.

"Professor Givens, I have to say I'm quite surprised to see you standing here with my ex."

Completely caught off guard by both Blaine's rude behavior as well as his inappropriate—and unnecessary—announcement, I gasped.

"That's neither my title, nor is it relevant, Blaine," I gritted through clenched teeth.

Blaine had the good sense to at least look chagrined, but mere seconds later it became apparent that it was all an act. He ducked his head briefly, glancing over at Rhone with a look in his eye that let me know he wasn't yet finished spouting foolishness.

"Considering how recently we were together, this seems a bit inappropriate."

The insinuation in his words shocked me. Of all the scenarios that I'd imagined of us seeing each other again, Blaine cosplaying a jealous asshole hadn't been in my top five. His behavior was throwing me for a loop.

"Hold on a minute," Rhone interrupted, his eyes widening as if he'd just understood what Blaine was trying to tell him. "You're Malina's ex? The one that —" He turned to me, an amused half-smile on his face. "*This* is him?"

A wave of embarrassment washed over me, and I nodded. It was just my luck that the man I was having fun with would know the one that had been the catalyst for our meeting in the first place.

Rhone winked at me and then held out a hand to Blaine, whose face was scrunched in confusion. "Man, let me shake your hand." Bewildered, Blaine grabbed Rhone's hand and pumped it twice.

"What..."

Rhone clapped Blaine on the bicep. "I just want to

thank you for sending Malina my way. We would never have met if it weren't for your words of discouragement."

Covering my mouth, I tried to stifle my giggle.

Trying to keep up with the conversation, Blaine shook his head. "Words of dis—wait, what do you mean '*send her your way*'? Are you two…seeing each other or something?" At that, he finally pinned his gaze on me.

Unsure how to answer that, my eyes swept over to Rhone's. There was a barely-there smirk at the corner of his mouth, which made me smile. He shot me another wink before turning back to Blaine.

"Something like that."

Blaine's eyebrows furrowed, and his eyes once again bounced between me and Rhone before he settled on me. He smiled, but his eyes were blank, and he leaned toward me.

"Well, don't forget what I told you." He'd lowered his voice, but not enough so that Rhone couldn't hear him, which seemed like his intention when he slid a sly glance over toward Rhone.

The volume in the room seemed to swell as my neck and face grew hot with embarrassment and shame. There was also anger. I was pissed that he'd chosen here of all places to bring that up. Gripping my champagne flute tightly so that I wouldn't reach up and slap him across the face, I smiled tightly.

"It's interesting that you felt the need to remind me of that tonight since we were together for two years, and yet you hadn't been bothered to mention it even once." Tilting my head to the side, I pinned him with a shrewd stare that caused him to shift in obvious discomfort. "I wonder what triggered your desire to be so…concerned all of a sudden."

Catching on to what we were likely talking about, Rhone smoothly wrapped an arm around my waist and tugged me toward him, bringing my back flush against his side. The enticing scent of his cologne and the comforting warmth of his body worked in tandem to ease the anger raging inside of me. Rhone then leaned down and nuzzled the soft skin beneath my earlobe, in an obviously possessive move that made Blaine's eyes narrow into slits. After a moment, he popped his head up as if just remembering that Blaine was standing in front of us.

"Oh, were you talking about that little oral issue?" My eyes widened and I canted my head to look at him, but he stared at Blaine who had begun to cough. I guess it was all fine and dandy when he was trying to diss me on the sly, but when it was addressed boldly, he couldn't handle it. Typical of a bully.

"Don't worry about that," Rhone instructed him. "That's been taken care of."

"Oh my lord," I murmured, torn between wanting to cover my face and enjoying the shock and confusion on Blaine's face entirely too much to block my vision.

"Wha—what do you mean?"

"Let's just say that I got Malina right." Dipping his chin, he met my eyes. "Ain't that right, baby?"

"You tell me," I responded softly.

Rhone had called me baby exactly three times, each of which when I was on my knees with his dick in my mouth. Hearing it now was like some sort of trigger word, causing my nipples to tighten and my pussy to start a steady thump inside of the tiny panties I wore underneath my dress. Rhone flicked his gaze back to Blaine, a smile on his face.

"Hey, man. Not everyone is called to teach, and there's no shame in that. I have to thank you though, for leaving it up to the professionals. Under my tutelage, Malina has blossomed. And now?" He met my eyes again, pulling that juicy bottom lip, that I now knew was soft and pliable, into his mouth and between his teeth. "Let's just say that I won't be letting her get away from me any time soon."

My body was buzzing with want, and the urge to pull his face to mine and guide his hand under my dress was strong. But we were at a party where most people were used to seeing me with Blaine, so instead of causing a scene, I turned to Blaine and offered him a bland smile. One day his ass would get what was coming to him for trying to embarrass me in public, but I had bigger and better things on my mind, and he just wasn't worth the time wasted.

"Goodbye, Blaine." I stepped out of the circle of Rhone's warmth, but before I could even chart my course, Blaine grabbed my wrist.

Trailing my gaze from his hand to his face, I lifted an eyebrow but otherwise stayed silent. Rhone's hand came to the small of my back and knowing he was there and ready to protect me again set the thumping between my thighs on hyperdrive.

"You look beautiful tonight," Blaine offered lamely.

I snorted. "I know. You should have led with that, instead of trying to bring me down a peg or whatever it is you called yourself doing."

He nodded, flicking his gaze to Rhone before coming back to me. "Can we talk for a moment?"

Frowning, I pulled out of his grasp and took a step back. I hadn't heard a peep out of Blaine in five weeks but today he wanted to talk? What were the odds?

"Nah. The only conversation I'm trying to have is with the mic in Rhone's pants."

Without waiting for Blaine to respond, I grabbed Rhone's hand and led him out of the living room and into the kitchen. It was mostly empty since the food and drinks were artfully arranged on the dining room table, which was perfect for my intentions. As soon as we were in there, I placed my flute on the countertop and spun to face Rhone, sliding my hands under his sweater and gripping his waist.

"I want to suck your dick. Right fucking now."

I expected his eyes to widen in shock, but he surprised me by lowering his head and leaning into me to drop a kiss on my neck.

"I hope you didn't think I was gon' say no. What did I tell you?"

Releasing a shuddering breath, I let my eyes fall closed.

"You said that the best head comes from a woman who wants to give it just as much as the man wants it."

Nodding, he leaned back to gaze down into my eyes. "I want to make sure you get everything you want."

His words made my pulse race and I dropped my gaze, finding the pattern of his sweater a wonderful distraction. Licking my lips, I shook my head.

"See, you need to watch what you say because when you say something like that, it makes me think you're talking about more than me activating the Throat Master 3000."

He laughed and leaned in once more, pressing a quick kiss to the corner of my mouth as he ran his hand down my arm. It seemed like it was an unconscious thing and I was helpless but to be enamored by it. "You make a man cry for mercy one time and now you got a nickname?"

"If winning one Super Bowl gets men called champions for the rest of their life, then I can surely have this."

Grinning, he nodded. "You're right. I'll give you that."

Silence descended upon us as we stood there, staring at one another. Parting my lips, I released a soft breath and just about whimpered when his eyes fell to my mouth. Just that quickly, I was reminded of my mission. Pulling my hands from under his sweater, I clasped his hand with mine and turned toward the double-paned, sliding glass doors that led to the pool and backyard. He followed my lead without hesitation, waiting while I pushed the door closed after we were on the patio and not asking any questions when I headed for the pool.

Right of the pool was a cabana and attached pool

house. Inside the small, one-room structure, which was for changing and showering before or after swimming, was an oversized, plush sectional which took up most of the room. I locked the door behind me and pulled Rhone over to the sofa. With my hands on his chest, all it took was a soft push for him to drop down to the seat, his legs spreading naturally.

I followed him down, lifting my dress above my knees so that I wouldn't wrinkle it as I settled in between his thighs. Instantly, he brought his hands to my arms, rubbing up and down my biceps almost absently.

"You signed up on JustOneNight with a goal in mind," he said after a moment, breaking the silence. "Do you feel like you were successful?"

As I unbuckled his pants and eased down his zipper, I nodded. "Absolutely. Thanks to your tutelage, I got exactly what I bargained for." Reaching inside of his pants, I pulled out his already hard dick before glancing up to meet his eyes. "Thanks, professor."

I bent to take him into my mouth, but he grabbed my locs in the circle of his hand and lifted me until we were face-to-face. The look in his eyes made the pounding in my heart radiate throughout my body until I could barely hear past the thud.

"What is it?" I whispered.

There was no one but Rhone and me in that pool house; nothing but the sound of our breathing and the distant thumping of bass coming from the main house accompanied us, but something about the way he was peering down at me felt monumental.

His pink tongue slipped out of his open mouth and rasped over his bottom lip. "I was wondering if it were possible for me to get something I wanted as well?"

Pushing out a breath, and wishing I could expel my nerves just as easily, I swallowed before asking, "What do you want?"

Those deep brown irises bored into me, yelling that I knew exactly what he wanted. And maybe I did, but I still wanted to hear it come out of those luscious ass lips.

"I want you."

"Me?" I asked because even though I'd heard him say it, I wanted to be sure that I wasn't imagining things.

"Nobody but," he quipped smartly, a slick grin on his sexy mouth.

"You know I had a boyfriend like five weeks ago, right?"

He shrugged. "Yeah. I also know your ex and know for a fact that you can do better."

Trying to be sassy, I quirked a brow, but I couldn't keep the pleased look off of my face. "Oh, are you better?"

"Yes, the fuck I am." Cupping my chin, he tugged me closer while leaning down to meet me halfway, pressing our lips together for a searing, possessive kiss that scorched me from top to bottom.

I clutched his thighs and pushed up onto my knees to get closer to him, leaning into the kiss and giving as much as I got. Rhone released my chin and slid his hands to my waist, heating my body wherever his hands touched me. Our tongues tangled sensuously, allowing me to taste the bourbon and bitters from the old fashioned he'd imbibed. Rhone tilted his head to one side in an attempt to deepen the kiss, but I pulled away before I decided to climb into his lap and take his dick into my body a different way than I'd originally intended.

"Okay," I whispered softly, chest heaving as I stared at him, loving the look of his wet and swollen lips and wishing we were at his house so that I could continue kissing him for hours.

"Okay?" he confirmed. "I can have you?"

I nodded, sliding back onto the floor and once again wrapping my hands around his steely erection, darting out my tongue to lick the bead of precum from the slit on his tip. "As long as you fuck my face first."

He swore, his thighs jerking up involuntarily. "Baby…"

A wicked grin tugged at my lips. "Call my baby again," I demanded.

Staring at me, his eyes heavy with lust and something else, Rhone licked his lips.

"Baby."

Groaning, I dropped my head, wetting my lips before taking him completely into my mouth. I gripped his base and squeezed as I bobbed up and down, hollowing my cheeks as I ascended. Saliva ran from my mouth, and I used the lubrication to put my nose in his lap, gagging when I went too far. Pushing air out of my nose, I lifted to the tip, preparing to try again, but Rhone grabbed my hair at my nape and lifted me completely off of his dick.

I stared at him, eyes blowout, feeling a trail of wetness run down my chin, knowing that my face was a nasty mess. Whatever caused him to stop me also kept him from being fazed by the state of my face. He shocked me by reaching under my arms and lifting me into his lap. My ass landed on his dick but I didn't have a minute to process what was going on before his tight grip on my locs was used to bring my face to his.

Our lips met in a clash of teeth and tongues. This kiss wasn't like the last one. That had been a declarative moment. Rhone was letting me know that we were going to take this thing further than a handful of blowjobs.

This kiss was nasty and full of the desperation of a man who was no longer in control. The man beneath me had taught me how to please a man while also recognizing my power, and at that moment, I realized the truth in his lessons.

The muffled sound of cheering followed by a loud boom made me wrench my mouth from his. Through the wooden blinds, I could see colorful lights dancing and I realized that those were the fireworks that indicated we'd entered into a new year. I turned back to Rhone who captured my lips again, this time in a brief, soft kiss.

"Happy new year," he whispered against my lips, causing me to grin.

"Happy new year, Rhone."

If this was how my new year began, with me in a beautiful man's lap, his tongue down my throat and his hard dick throbbing against my panty-clad pussy, then it was quite obvious this year was going to be a very happy one indeed.

ABOUT THE AUTHOR

Chencia C. Higgins is just a girl from Texas writing about sassy, southern women finding love. With a multitude of titles under her belt, she has made it her mission to create stories in which Black women are loved out loud. In 2019 she won a Romance Slam Jam Emma award for her debut paranormal romance, Janine: His True Alpha. When she isn't hunkered down in her writing cave, Chencia can be found with her nose in a book (or two, or three), saving recipes on Pinterest, and traveling as much as possible with her family.

To be informed about future releases, events, and happenings, visit her website.
www.therealchencia.com